THE GOLDEN COMPASS™

LYRA'S WORLD

KAY WOODWARD

ISBN-13: 978-0-545-01617-9
ISBN-10: 0-545-01617-7

12 11 10 9 8 7 6 5 4 3 2 1   7 8 9 10 11 12/0

Editorial Director: Lisa Edwards
Project Manager: Neil Kelly
Project Editor: Laura Milne
Designer: Aja Bongiorno
Printed in Singapore
First printing, November 2007

SCHOLASTIC INC.

New York   Toronto   London   Auckland   Sydney
Mexico City   New Delhi   Hong Kong   Buenos Aires

❧ Lyra ❧

Lyra Belacqua is twelve years old. She isn't afraid to say what she thinks—or to tell lies. She skips lessons, hates to dress up, and is eager for adventure. Lyra has lived in Oxford ever since she was very young. Lyra never knew her parents and would like to learn more about them.

Lyra lives in a world that *looks* like ours, but is totally different.

❧ Dæmons ❧

In Lyra's world, a person's soul lives outside their body.
It takes the form of a dæmon—a talking animal. A child's
dæmon can change into any animal. But as the child grows
older, the dæmon will settle into one form. Dæmons
accompany their people wherever they go. *No one*
must come between a person and their dæmon.

Lyra's dæmon is called
Pantalaimon, or Pan
for short. He loves Lyra
more than anyone else in
the world. He takes
many forms, including
an ermine, a wildcat,
a moth, and a bird.

❧ Roger ❧

Lyra's best friend is named Roger Parslow. He works in
the kitchens at Jordan College. Roger tries to stay out
of trouble, but Lyra can always talk him into exploring!
Together, they visit the parts of the college that are
strictly off-limits. One day Lyra makes Roger a promise:
If anything bad ever happens to him, she will come to
his rescue.

Roger tells Lyra about
the Gobblers. They
are people who steal
children. No one
knows who they are or
why they do it.

❧ Lord Asriel ❧

Lord Asriel is Lyra's uncle. He's an explorer. He often goes away on long trips. On his latest adventure he visited the North Pole. There he learned about strange particles called Dust. He also found a hole at the top of the world that leads to other worlds. Lyra dreams of following him when he returns north.

Asriel's dæmon is a snow leopard named Stelmaria.

❧ Jordan College ❧

Lord Asriel brought Lyra to this Oxford college when she was very young. It is the only home she has ever known. Lord Asriel asked the Master of the college to bring her up as a lady. He has not had much success.

Lyra loves walking on the roofs of Jordan College with her friend Roger Parslow.

The Master is in charge of Lyra's education and safety. When Lyra leaves Oxford, he gives her a truth-telling device called an alethiometer.

To ask the alethiometer a question, a person moves the three hands so they each point to different symbols around the edge. Then, while they hold the question in their mind, the needle will spin round the dial to reveal the answer.

❧ The Alethiometer ❧

The alethiometer looks like a big, fancy, golden pocket watch. It is also known as the Golden Compass. Instead of showing the way North like a normal compass, its needle points toward Truth. The alethiometer can only be read by someone with a very special talent—Lyra is one of these people.

✎ Mrs. Coulter ✎

Mrs. Coulter is very pretty and very powerful. She charms everyone she meets, including Lyra. Her dæmon is the Golden Monkey. He is sneaky and sometimes unkind. It is difficult to figure out Mrs. Coulter's real plans. But one thing is for sure—she will get whatever she wants.

If the Golden Monkey has a name, then Mrs. Coulter keeps it very secret.

The Magisterial Seat looms
high above the city of London.
This huge building is the home
of the mighty Magisterium.

⨳ Lyra's London ⨳

For Lyra, London is a city full of new experiences: shopping for clothes, going to fancy parties, and meeting all of Mrs. Coulter's friends. Lyra even gets to stay in Mrs. Coulter's apartment. But there is danger there, too.

Mrs. Coulter carries out her secret work from her beautiful apartment.

ᕙ The Gyptians ᕗ

The Gyptians are smugglers and traders. They travel by water, making a living as they go. Although they appear rough and tough, they are very caring people. When their children are stolen by the Gobblers, they vow to do anything to rescue them. This includes spying, fighting, killing, and even traveling to the ends of the earth.

Billy Costa is one of
the first children to be
kidnapped. His mother,
Ma Costa, takes Lyra
under her wing.

Gyptians prefer to travel by water rather than by land. At sea, the Gyptians use a huge, oceangoing ship called the *Noorderlicht*.

❧ The Elders ❧

John Faa is the king of the Gyptians. He is very big, very old, and very wise. Farder Coram has been John Faa's friend and advisor for many years. These highly respected Gyptian elders offer to help and protect Lyra.

❧ Serafina Pekkala ❧

Serafina Pekkala is a Witch Queen. Even though she has lived for more than three hundred years, she still looks young and beautiful. Like all witches, Serafina is able to fly. She believes that Lyra will play an important role in the war which is to come.

Long ago, Farder Coram saved Serafina Pekkala's life. They would do anything to help each other.

❧ Iorek Byrnison ❧

Iorek Byrnison is a huge, powerful Ice Bear. He was once a king, but he was cast out of his kingdom—on the island of Svalbard. Lyra helps Iorek to become great again. In return, he pledges to always be her friend and protector.

Ice Bears are warriors and metalworkers. Ice Bears make their own armor using sky-iron from the falling stars that land on Svalbard.

❧ Lee Scoresby ❧

This tall Texan flies his airship for a living, carrying out risky, well-paid jobs such as spying and fighting. Lee Scoresby is a great friend of Iorek the Ice Bear. They have worked together in the past and trust each other.

The boat-shaped cockpit of Lee's airship is supported by two silver double balloons, which are held in place by many ropes.

Lee's dæmon is Hester, a hare. She has keen hearing and a relaxed, laid-back nature.

Like everywhere else in Lyra's world, Bolvangar uses anbaric power. This is like electricity. But instead of producing a harsh glare, anbaric lights give off a softer glow.

❧ Bolvangar ❧

In the middle of an icy wasteland stands the Experimental Station. The witches call it Bolvangar. A collection of low, white buildings, it is home to doctors and nurses who carry out experiments on children. No one knows what these experiments are—all they know is that once a child is taken away, they are never seen again. . . .

Ragnar Sturlusson

If Iorek Byrnison is big, then Ragnar Sturlusson is enormous. He's the new king of the Ice Bears—and he looks it. Ragnar wears many jewels and his long claws are decorated with gold.

Ragnar Sturlusson wants one thing more than any other. He wants a dæmon. The Ice Bear even carries a human-shaped doll around with him. He pretends it is his dæmon.

❧ The Northern Lights ❧

At the very top of Lyra's world, red, green, and blue light dances across the night sky. This magnificent, shimmering display is known as the Northern Lights, although some call it the Aurora. The Northern Lights hide the gateway to a billion other worlds, where anything is possible.